The Large Rock
and The Little Yew

Gregory M. Ahlijian (signature)

THE
LARGE ROCK
AND THE
LITTLE YEW

A SHORT STORY ABOUT COURAGE, PERSEVERANCE,
SELF-RESPECT, AND HOPE

by
Gregory M. Ahlijian

Copyright © 2010 by Gregory M. Ahlijian
Illustrations by Janna Roselund
Cover and book design by Hannah Bontrager

Little Yew Tree
www.littleyewtree.com
Eugene, Oregon

10   9   8   7   6   5   4   3   2

This book is set in Adobe Jenson Pro.

ISBN 978-0-692-01158-4

Printed in China

Dedicated to all the children who walk
the peaceful, wooded trails at
Jasper Mountain School

FOREWORD

The Large Rock and the Little Yew is more than a metaphorical tale for children. It is a story of survival, accepting one's challenges, and achieving through determination and willpower. The best part is that the story is true! Other than the anthropomorphic dialogue, the little yew tree in fact did what the story describes—it succeeded against all the odds because of its hardships, not in spite of them.

The author, obviously a lover of trees and little humans, chose a living specimen to demonstrate a most unexpected and magnificent outcome. What the author correctly implies is that the hardships of the little yew tree propelled it to the heights of full realization, even beyond the other trees with fewer hardships to overcome. It is a story that effortlessly weaves in lessons for a successful life, and not just for yew trees. The author is saying something important to children through a true story that will draw their interest. Every great story has a moral, and here the moral is that despite the hardships every child encounters, whether child abuse or other less-than-ideal growing conditions, it is the strength and resiliency that comes from the unfair struggle itself that can be the catalyst to the greatness God intends for us all.

— Dave Ziegler
Executive Director, Jasper Mountain
Jasper, Oregon

Doom

Once upon a time ever so long ago, a tiny yew tree seed happened to nestle itself quite by accident in the fissure of a large rock. How it got there remains a mystery. Perhaps the wind carried the small seed from a nearby tree to its new resting place. Or perhaps a forest mouse or bird, having found the large rock an ideal place to have lunch, set the seed down to eat its fleshy red pulp—only to have it roll away out of reach into the rock's hollow. In any case, it doesn't matter how the yew seed got there. What is important is that it was seemingly trapped and certain for doom.

Or perhaps a forest mouse or bird, having found the large rock an ideal place to have lunch, set the seed down.

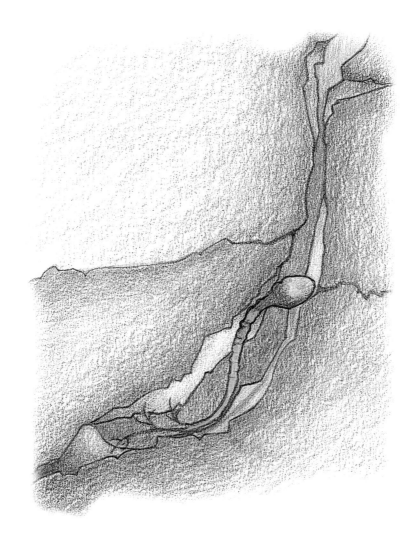

The outer shell of the seed opened and a curious root appeared.

Harsh Realities

T hrough cold winter days and nights the yew seed lay within the dark and dingy narrow-walled split of the large rock. Week upon week passed, and it lay quietly alone. Its future couldn't possibly be hopeful.

After several months passed and the cold winter turned to the promise of spring, the yew seed awoke in its dark, creviced home. The outer shell of the seed opened and a curious root appeared. This one single tiny root began to search for the comfort of some good, warm soil to nourish itself, but all it could feel were the surrounding steep, hard, and cold walls of the split rock. The yew seedling didn't know what to make of it. Certainly this wasn't the ideal setting for such a young tree. However uneasy it may have felt, the little seedling bravely decided to further explore its uninviting environment. The little seedling extended its root a little deeper along the wall of the rock's fissure and discovered, quite to its delight, a pocket of soil just large enough to sustain it.

Within days, the seedling gained a little strength and began extending its tender, supple stem from the depths of the dark, cold rock walls upward toward a warm and inviting ray of sunlight.

CONFLICT AND STRUGGLE

Alas," the little yew thought to itself, "If only I could reach that ray of sunlight I so desperately need. With the moisture contained in this pocket of soil, I think I might have a chance to make it."

The little yew gathered all its courage and strength. It dug its thirsty root a little deeper into the small pocket of trapped soil. It lifted its stem toward the sunlight. With all its might and determination, the little yew began ever so slowly to rise above the surrounding wall of rock to bask in the warmth of full sunlight. After all, it was a matter of life or death.

The large rock, feeling all the commotion from the little yew's efforts, suddenly awoke from its somber sleep and became very angry.

"What's going on down there?" the large rock shouted to the little yew. "I'm used to lying here in peace! The tickling of your root and stem is annoying me to no end!"

The little yew was quite startled to hear the vociferous complaints of the large rock. All the little yew was doing was trying to survive. Surely the large rock would understand.

The little yew innocently replied to the large rock, "I found myself in this very unwelcoming place due to no fault of my own. All I'm trying to do is survive and make something of myself."

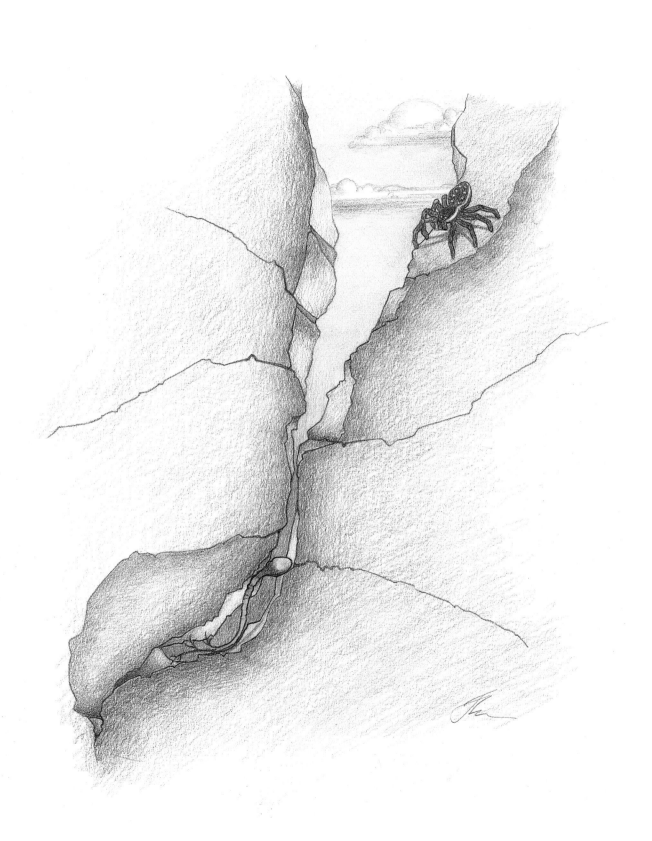

"If only I could reach that ray of sunlight I so desperately need," the little yew thought.

"The drifting snow will cover you for weeks at a time," said the large rock.

On hearing the little yew's plea, the large rock became furious. "Survive? Survive? Make something of yourself? How dare you have such foolish dreams! Don't you know what awaits you? In a few weeks it will be summer. The sun will beat down upon you. It will get very hot and dry. The only moisture your tiny root will find will be trapped deep within my crevice. You will no doubt shrivel up and die."

The large rock suddenly became silent, but only for a moment. Then it began again. "And if by some miracle you make it through the hot, dry summer, even more harsh weather awaits you! Come winter, the cold winds will blow. The drifting snow will cover you for weeks at a time. You will surely freeze to death! If summer's scorching heat doesn't get you, winter's icy grip surely will! Listen to me. Your challenge is too great. Don't you know it is much easier to be a rock? For a rock does not need sunlight or water or nourishment from the soil. It just lies on the ground and does nothing, without a worry in the world."

Deliberation

What the large rock had just told the little yew was all new and very frightening. The little yew didn't know quite what to make of all that the big, grouchy rock had put forth, for it had never experienced the extremes of weather.

The little yew again paused and gathered itself, remaining silent for a long time, thinking. "Is the large rock right? Have I no chance?" it wondered.

The little yew reflected back on its short life and the struggles it had already endured. It seemed that from what the large rock had said, nothing lay ahead but more struggles. Finally, after seemingly pondering its troubles for hours, the little yew gathered the courage to reply to the large rock.

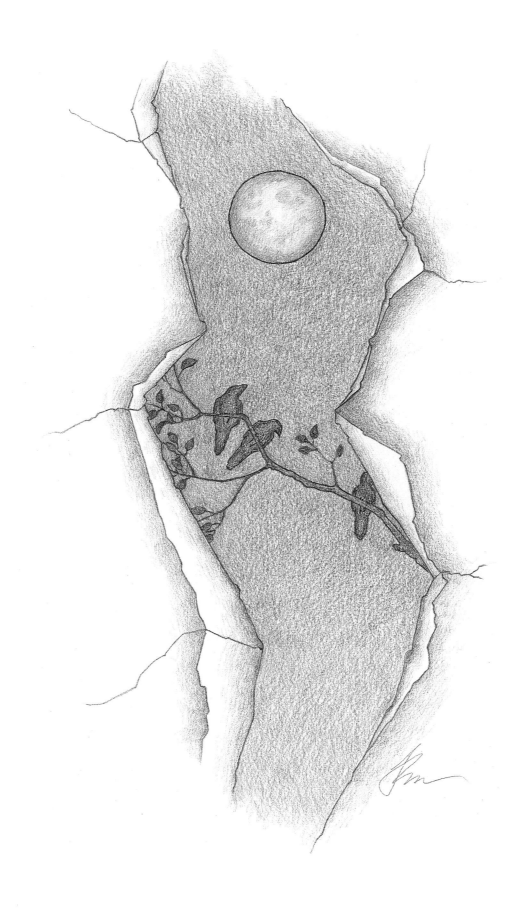

"Is the large rock right? Have I no chance?" the yew tree wondered.

"I am unlike the baobab tree!" said the little yew.

Unlike the Baobab Tree

The little yew reached deep within itself and, with a good measure of belief, declared to the large rock, "I am unlike the baobab tree!"

"The what tree?" the large rock angrily responded.

"The baobab tree. You know, the 'upside-down' tree," the little yew softly replied, hoping to calm down the angry large rock.

"I know of no 'upside-down' tree," the large rock answered, now curious. "After all, I'm a rock, and a rather large and handsome one at that, don't you forget."

The little yew cautiously began again to address the large rock. "Now that you've calmed down a bit, I will tell you about the baobab tree." (It isn't common knowledge, but trees of one species instinctively know about trees of another species. It's a survival thing.)

After a short pause to get its thoughts in order, the little yew explained. "The baobab tree is a very large tree with root-like branches that grows in Africa. It is often wider than it is tall, and it has the special ability to store huge amounts of water in the cavities of its enormous trunk. To native Africans, it truly became a 'tree of life,' for they depend on it for water during periods of drought."

To native Africans the baobab tree became a "tree of life," for it could store water in the cavities of its enormous trunk.

"In addition, the fibrous bark of the baobab is used for making ropes and sacks, and it can even be woven to make cloth," the little yew tree continued.

"However, as legend has it, it was not a very happy tree. It complained to God that it wasn't pleased with the way it looked, for it could see the reflection of other trees in the pond by which it grew. The baobab became jealous of the neighboring trees, thinking their leaves, bark, and flowers were much prettier than its own. The baobab's constant complaints made God very upset. The baobab could not appreciate the fact that God made the baobab a unique tree and placed it to grow by a lovely pond where it could see the reflection of surrounding trees. It would therefore never be lonely and always have plenty of water to drink—and, by the way, baobabs soak up a lot of water.

"Finally, after growing very tired of hearing the baobab's endless complaints and with much consideration, God returned to the baobab, picked it up, and replanted it—upside-down in the earth. The baobab could no longer see its reflection or those of the other trees. The baobab paid a big price to learn an important lesson."

"What does this all have to do with your predicament?" the impatient large rock interrupted. "I find myself with a yew tree growing out of me, and you ramble on about some tree in Africa growing upside-down. What foolishness! I'm getting quite tired of it all. Don't you know that I'm used to leading a very monotonous life here? All this activity, tickling, and talk of a baobab tree is extremely annoying. It's got to stop at once! Do you hear me?"

The baobab became jealous of the neighboring trees, thinking their leaves, bark, and flowers were much prettier than its own.

RESOLVE

The little yew didn't know quite how to respond to the angry demands of the impatient large rock. After all, the little yew was just starting out in life and in a predicament not to its choosing or liking. The little yew was scared, its feelings were hurt, and, on top of it all, it was forced to deal with a very large and angry rock. Ordinarily it would be hard enough to make something of itself in life and grow to become a yew of great importance. Here it found itself having to do it all from what seemed an impossible state of affairs. Of all the places to be starting life's journey, this wasn't anything even close to normal.

Understandably, the little yew again became very quiet and gave the seriousness of its plight much thought. Luckily for it, the large rock had calmed down and gone to sleep for the night. In the quiet of that late spring evening, the little yew reflected back to the baobab tree and what it was trying to explain to the large rock before being so rudely interrupted by the rock's angry outburst.

Unlike the baobab, the little yew smartly decided that it would be best not to waste valuable time and energy complaining about the situation where it found itself. The baobab was a unique tree with much to be proud of, but couldn't see it. The little yew was determined to celebrate all of its uniqueness and wisely use all the gifts God had given it.

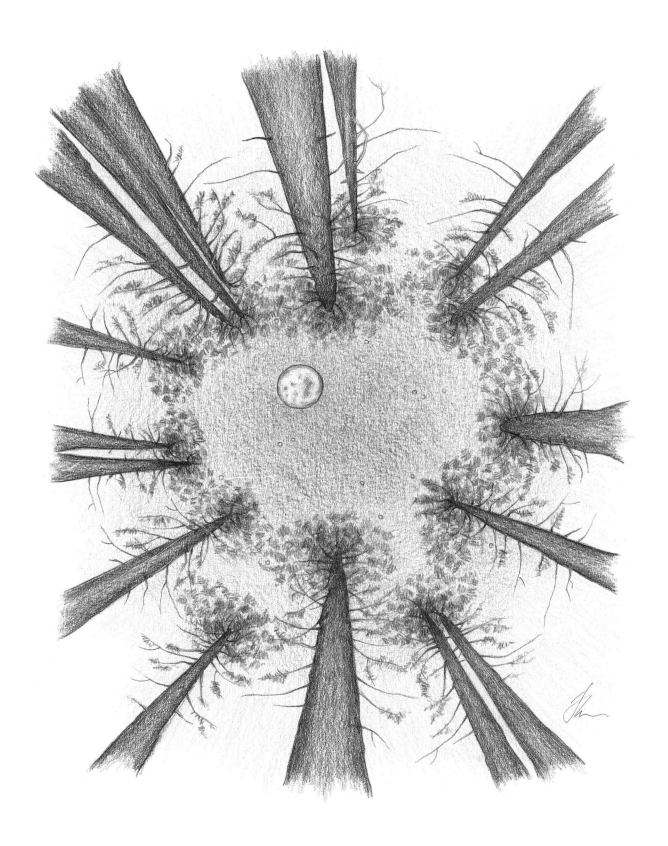

In the quiet of that late spring evening, the little yew reflected on what it was trying to explain to the large rock.

The greatest joy in life is found in small acts of kindness and giving.

The little yew instinctively knew that to ancient people, the yew tree was known as the guardian of time and was a symbol of everlasting life. The little yew, however, had even more to be proud of. Recalling the angry large rock's exaggerated warnings of winter's frigid, stinging bite, the little yew felt confident that its evergreen leaves would keep it warm even during winter's coldest nights. The little yew's concerns were fast fading. Pride and a sense of belonging were confidently growing within it.

The little yew imagined itself a few years older, after working very hard to reach one of its goals—bearing the flame-red berries that would be nestled among its short, needle-like leaves. The little yew could easily picture itself as a handsome sentinel of the forest, with plenty of winged and four-legged friends stopping by to enjoy the bounty the little yew would provide. This thought was especially pleasing to the little yew, for it instinctively knew that the greatest joy in life is found in small acts of kindness and giving. (This may be a difficult life lesson to learn, especially when you are young and think you have no gifts to share. Remember that trees are very wise, especially yews.)

With this sense of purpose, the little yew became even more determined in its calling, for its forest friends would be dependent on it not only for food, but for shelter as well. The little yew was very pleased that it would become an important provider. A strength of spirit and determination grew deep within the little yew's soul. The little yew decided it would confidently and convincingly address the large rock in the morning, when the large rock awoke. Exhausted, but not discouraged, the little yew fell soundly asleep.

Self-Respect and Confidence

In the early morning, as the sun's warm rays shined upon the large rock and the little yew, the forest came to life again. The large rock, upon awaking, said to the little yew in a much calmer voice, "Are you still here? I thought I felt the tickle of your root."

The little yew, with full command, exclaimed, "You're a rock, I'm a tree. Neither of us is going anywhere!"

"Now hold on," the large rock responded, its voice slightly raised. "Don't get smart with me. I told you yesterday, you may recall, that there is no way you're going to make it."

The little yew, showing no outward sign of being frightened in the slightest degree, exclaimed, "No! I'm tired of the disrespect you've shown me thus far. The more you tell me I can't do something, the more resolve I'll have to prove you wrong! I'll show you that it will be a big mistake not to believe in me!"

Understandably, this response utterly shocked the large rock. For once, it was taken aback. No one in the forest had ever spoken to the large rock with such confidence and belief. Certainly not the curious forest fox and rabbits that would scamper upon the large rock to scan the forest floor, nor the many birds that would alight on the large rock to rest for a spell.

No one in the forest had ever spoken to the large rock with such confidence and belief . . . not the curious forest fox.

No, not even the chubby brown bear had ever spoken to the large rock with so much conviction.

No, not even the large buck with its enormous antlers nor the chubby brown bear that would occasionally stop by and use the large rock as a scratching post—much to the large rock's dismay—had ever spoken with so much conviction.

Sensing that the large rock had been taken completely by surprise, the little yew confidently continued and politely explained to the large rock, "All I want is to be given a chance to grow up and join the ranks of all the other proud yews that have preceded me." The little yew further explained to the large rock that it would rely on the gifts God had thoughtfully given it. With help from the soil for nourishment, sunlight for energy, and water to quench its thirsty roots, all the little yew wanted was the opportunity to ground itself—to spread its roots into the rich fertile soil that lay just beyond its reach. The little yew pictured itself extending its limbs broadly and standing majestically among the other trees in the forest.

The large rock, having heard all of this put so clearly before it, gained a great deal of respect for the little yew, for it was apparent that the little yew had much self-respect as well as respect for all the other important things essential for a happy and healthy life. The large rock assessed the recent developments and rightly thought to itself that it didn't have much of a choice in this matter any longer. The large rock and the little yew made the best of their dilemma and agreed to peacefully coexist. After all, what other logical choice did they have?

Epilogue

Throughout the following years, the little yew worked intently and grew to eventually spread its roots far beyond the big rock. The little yew bravely faced gale-force winds, blizzard snows, the deep chill of ice, and the droughts of many a long summer. Year after year, the little yew measured up to the fury of storms and, though sometimes wounded, was able to withstand all that Mother Nature brought upon it. The little yew slowly grew to become the most majestic and respected tree in the forest.

And the large rock? The very angry large rock that didn't want anything to do with the little yew? Well, it is now also very famous, for people travel from all over the world to Wakehurst in the United Kingdom to view the sight of a large limestone rock encased within the roots of this awe-inspiring yew.

So you see, without the will of the yew tree, the large rock would have remained just another rock in the forest, never to be given a second thought. The yew tree, on the other hand, in a less challenging location would have grown to be just another tree in the forest. It would never pique one's curiosity to stop and ask: "How did this happen?" The yew tree grew to become majestic and respected not in spite of the large angry rock but because the added challenges it faced and chose to conquer enabled it to achieve a deeper level of self-discovery, courage, perseverance, self-respect, and hope.

Isn't it funny how life plays itself out?

The little yew further explained to the large rock that it would rely on the gifts God had thoughtfully given it.

The yew tree grew to become majestic and respected not in spite of the large angry rock
but because of the added challenges it faced.

Photograph: Douglas Malkasian

You can visit the large rock and the no-longer-so-little yew tree at Wakehurst, United Kingdom.

Author's Note

The inspiration for this allegory originated with all the children at Jasper Mountain School I've had the honor to mentor, especially the children in Julie Delperdang's class with whom I have the privilege of sharing my love of trees.

To Mikayla, James, Alex K., Mariah, Jake, Amy, John, Alex C., Christen, Stevon, and Noah
Also to Joe, Zack, and Dillon

Thank you for your trust,
Greg

Acknowledgments

I am grateful to the following people for their contributions:

Randy Sprick, Ph.D., Educational Consultant, Pacific Northwest Publishing—Thank you for making the resources of Pacific Northwest Publishing available to me to help me in realizing my goal. Historically, our business association has been centered on friendship and trust, and this venture has been no different.

The wonderful and talented team at Pacific Northwest Publishing, including Chief Operating Officer Matt Sprick, editor Sara Ferris, graphic designers Hannah Bontrager and Natalie Conaway, and all other staff members who contributed their talents to this project. In every aspect it has been a pleasure working with you. You have graciously provided me with the guidance and expertise to make a dream come true.

Dave Ziegler, Ph.D., Executive Director, Jasper Mountain, who has guided me and allowed me to navigate my way around the facility and discover opportunities to use any creative talent I may have to effectively teach and mentor children. This book is a manifestation of one of those opportunities.

Doug Malkasian, a friend I have had the pleasure of knowing for more than 43 years. A friend who, without hesitation, agreed to take an excursion to Wakehurst to photograph the yew tree during a vacation trip he and his wife, Ann, took to London. Thank you—the inclusion of the yew tree photo really brings the story to life.

Brian Lanker, an extremely talented and award-winning photographer and author, and his wife Lynda, an accomplished portrait artist. Friends of mine for more than thirty years, Brian and Lynda were helpful with design suggestions and guidance.

Jasper Mountain: A Place of Positive Change

After years of thought and planning, a treatment center for young children opened in the foothills of the Cascade mountains in Oregon in 1982. This center was designed to address the problem of helping the most difficult children heal from their past problems and become healthy and happy children, teens, and eventually adults. Because it was a pretty tall order to bring the most challenging children together in one place and work with them, this effort was considered an experiment from the very beginning.

The experiment was essentially to take children who either were not exposed to environments where their needs were met or were unable to accept what was offered and give them a world that was safe, healthy, healing, and fun as well. For children to heal, there must be ample opportunities to learn and to have fun. These are found in abundance at Jasper Mountain. Regardless of the priorities of our society and regardless of good or bad economic times, difficult children have always demanded attention. Jasper Mountain has had no shortage of children to work with.

The environment has always been important to the goal of health and healing for these children. A beautiful location provides forests, rivers, waterfalls, wildlife, clean water, fresh air, and room to explore. From the beginning of the program thirty years ago, adults have come to the property and remarked that it felt like a healing place. In this environment, personal healing occurs every day of the year for thousands of deserving children.

Jasper Mountain is an intensive, specialized mental health facility complete with many types of sophisticated therapy. It is also a working family ranch with chores to attend to, animals to feed, and ample time for recreation. The combination of intensive psychological therapy and a treatment family is one reason for the success of Jasper Mountain. This once-humble experiment has grown to where it is today, with an international reputation for positive outcomes for even the most difficult and damaged children.

This work has attracted wonderful staff and caring and skilled volunteers to be a part of a village where children learn to move on from the past and embrace possibilities for a bright and successful future. Jasper Mountain is a place of positive change for the children and the adults who come to this special place. More information is available at www.jaspermountain.org.

About the Author

Greg Ahlijian is a volunteer at Jasper Mountain Center, where he teaches children about nature, trees, character development, and poetry.

He has been self-employed in the field of arboriculture for more than 30 years. In 1976, he published a book of prose and poetry titled *Reflections In My Quiet Hours*. Greg has shown his abstract oil paintings in art galleries along the West Coast during the 1970s and has traveled to Africa several times to photograph the continent's wildlife, in particular his favorite—elephants.

In regard to his teaching at Jasper Mountain Center, he says: "My goal is to inspire the child's sense of self-worth by creatively and effectively teaching the components of good character and illustrating them with examples present in everyday activities. It is my hope that every child leaving Jasper Mountain School will be given a copy of the book, including personalized wishes from staff. The book will thus become a keepsake of an important time and place in the development of the child. To all other children and adults this book may reach, I hope you find reading pleasure and merit in its lessons."

Proceeds from this book will be donated to the children at Jasper Mountain Center. As Greg has stated: "It's their story."

About the Illustrator

Janna Roselund's love of nature, study of lucid dreaming, and interest in literature, folklore, and mythology are all evident in her drawing, painting, writing, and design. In her work, she tries to discover and achieve as much as possible of originality and technical excellence.

A native Oregonian, Janna was raised in rural Douglas County. She began her professional career working in jewelry design and fabrication. She has also given art lessons to adults and children, designed lettering and signs, produced hand-colored black-and-white photography, and written five children's books and numerous short stories. Currently, she is producing a series of oil paintings for gallery exhibition and working as a freelance designer and writer.